"The Faith of a Bride"
Prequel to the "Women of Faith" Series
By L.A. Pattillo

This is a work of fiction. Similarities to real people, places, or events are entirely coincidental.

THE FAITH OF A BRIDE

First edition. May 27, 2019.

Copyright © 2019 L.A. Pattillo.

Written by L.A. Pattillo.

DEDICATION

To my soulmate.
None of my dreams would
be possible without you.
Thank you for your encouragement
your kindness and your
never-ending support.

ACKNOWLEDGEMENTS

A big thank you to Shaela Odd
at Blue Water Books for the
beautiful cover! You truly
are an artist.

CHAPTER 1

Tabitha wiped the thin beads of sweat dripping down her forehead with the sleeve of her dress. The summer sun beat down on the city of Ammonihah with unrelenting force and even her loose, layered robes could not keep her cool from its excessive heat. She paused a moment in her work to study the town square surrounding her.

Dozens of women were gathered at the well where Tabitha sat, gossiping, laughing and working. The individual conversations were indistinguishable as the women attempted to talk over each other. Their voices mingled with the tinkling of gold bracelets and other jewelry each time they waved their arms to punctuate their words.

Like many of the women there, Tabitha had come to collect a jug of water to take back to her father's household. The walk, even in the heat, was a welcome reprieve from her demanding mother and other household chores.

Tabitha loved watching people as they paraded around the town square. Each person had their own lives, yet all lived together in one city. Merchants hocked their wares, men stood in groups loudly debating the latest controversy, and children played with sticks while their laughter rang through the alleys. In one corner, bright flashes of color jumped through the air as a group of unmarried girls danced and waved scarves in merriment. The men standing close by plucked strings and blew their instruments while smiling at the display the girls created.

The sounds of a chaotic market could be heard across the square and Tabitha's eyes wandered to the busy stalls as people bickered and fought for better prices. Taking a deep breath, she let her fingers skim along the surface of the fountain where she sat, the cool, wetness of the water created a stark contrast to the dry, dusty air surrounding her. She smiled as she watched the younger girls giggle and point at the young men parading through the streets in an effort to be noticed, but her smile quickly dropped when a sharp pang hit her heart.

I am well past the age to marry, yet I still reside at my father's home. She had a fleeting desire to be a young girl again, one who batted her eyelashes and shared a secretive grin with a handsome man. But those days seemed far behind her while her future remained uncertain. To her knowledge, no man had come seeking a conference with her father and her father seemed in no hurry to push her from his house.

With a weary sigh, she gathered her heavy, rough pottery, lifting it carefully to keep from spilling, and made her way back to her father's dwelling.

After arriving home, she noticed the servants bustling about in an unusually eager manner. Tabitha paused in the doorway, frowning. "What has happened?" she asked one of the women sweeping.

The middle-aged woman glanced about before speaking quietly. "We were told to prepare for a guest, Miss. I know nothing more."

"Thank you," Tabitha said absently as she ventured further into the house. She was relieved to find her mother in the kitchen when she went to drop off the water she carried.

"Mother, what has happened? The servants speak of a guest, but no one knows who is coming."

"Ah, you are finally home." Tabitha's mother, Miriam, bustled over to her. "Come, we must make you ready."

"Ready for what?" Tabitha asked over her shoulder while her mother shepherded her into her bedroom.

"Wash." Miriam demanded. "I have left oils to rub on your hair and skin. We want you at your best."

"Mother, who is coming? And why must I look my best?" Tabitha's voice had risen as her frustration mounted. She immediately snapped her mouth shut and looked down when her mother raised an imperious eyebrow.

"Daughter." Miriam's voice dripped heavy with disappointment. "You have been taught better."

"You are right, Mother. I am sorry." Tabitha looked up from under her long, dark lashes. "But please, will you not tell me what is happening?"

In a moment of uncharacteristic softness, Miriam sighed and stepped closer, putting her hand on Tabitha's cheek. She gave a small smile and rubbed her thumb over the creamy, youthful skin of her daughter. "It seems only yesterday you were unable to walk, and now your father wishes to present you to a man."

Tabitha's eyes widened, and she gasped. Nerves skittered down her spine at the thought of marrying and leaving her family. *Was it not but a few moments ago I was lamenting being older than the other girls? And yet now I feel fear at the thought of leaving. How can this be?*

"If all goes well, you are to meet your future father-in-law soon. You will serve him tonight at dinner."

Tabitha frowned. "Will I not meet my betrothed?"

Miriam clucked her tongue and scowled. "You do not wish to appear too eager, Daughter. You will meet your husband in time." With that, Miriam swept from the room and left Tabitha alone.

Slowly, mechanically, Tabitha pulled off her layers of robes until she could sufficiently wash the sweat and dust from her body. Her mind presented dozens of scenarios, some wonderful, some terrifying.

Did father approach this man? Or did he approach father? Will I like him? Will he like me? This last thought caused her to stop her preparations. After a moment, Tabitha shook her head and continued getting herself ready. She knew that love was not common among marriages, but she couldn't stop her heart from hoping to find it in her own. Her parents were not in love, but they owned respect for each other. "That is all I can ask for," Tabitha murmured to herself.

A knock on the door caused her to look up. "Who is it? Tabitha asked.

"Are you ready?" her mother asked through the doorway.

"Yes, come in." Tabitha finished putting on her head dress as Miriam walked in the door.

Tears filled Miriam's eyes. "You are so beautiful." Walking over to her daughter she began to fuss with Tabitha's outfit. "We must put on your jewelry."

Tabitha grabbed her mother's hands and held them close to her heart. "I'm nervous, Mother. Can you tell me nothing more about who is coming tonight?"

Miriam squeezed Tabitha's hands. "All I know is that your father was very proud of the possible match. I believe he must be a man similar in station to your father to be so excited. Of course, we know he will be taken with your beauty but the rest is up to your father." Miriam sniffed. "Come, let us put on the finishing touches."

Once her mother left, Tabitha sat, fidgeting in her room, waiting for her father to call her out. *Taken by my beauty? Does Mother really believe that? If my beauty was so great, why have I not had other offers?*

A knock sounded down the hall and Tabitha thought her heart might pound out of her chest. Cautiously, she crept toward her door, resting her ear against it. Low, mumbled voices were the only sound she could hear. Frustration bubbled inside her at being kept ignorant. *Is it not my life that is being discussed? Why do women have no say in these matters?*

Biting her lip and forcing her breath to stay steady and quiet, Tabitha eased the door open. Carefully, she slid into the hallway and moved along the wall until she reached the opening to the front room. She kept her movements slow and deliberate, so as not to disturb the layers of gold hanging heavy on her chest and hands. The stone wall at her back felt cool against her flushed skin as she pressed herself into the shadows; straining to hear what was being said.

"Your lineage is, obviously, unmatched," Tabitha's father said, a smile evident in his voice.

"As is yours," a deep voice replied, sounding strong and firm. "The match would be one that would benefit both families."

"Indeed," Tabitha's father, Luram, murmured. She could imagine him stroking his bearded chin as he studied the other man. Her father was a well-known, shrewd businessman. Although he had come from a wealthy family, his keen mind had pushed their family into even greater riches and status. He had already seen all his other children into advantageous marriages and Tabitha knew, deep down, that he would do the same for her.

"I hear your daughter's beauty is known throughout the city." A note of skepticism could be heard in the stranger's tone. "If that is so, then why have you not married her off already?"

What? Tabitha nearly groaned at the comment. Although she knew she was not homely, Tabitha had never considered herself a great beauty. *Great beauties are the women who have men clamoring to watch them dance in the city center. They are the ones who smile and men stumble over the cobblestones.* She shook her head. *What will this man do when he finds I am not what he expected?*

"Tabitha, is my youngest daughter. Can you blame an old man for being sentimental? She is a good and dutiful daughter and although she will make someone a good wife, it has been hard to think of having her gone." Tabitha's cheeks and heart warmed at her father's words. She could hear him settle himself on his chair. "As you know, I was not blessed with any sons. Once Tabitha is married, it will leave my house empty. Maybe I held on longer than I should." The rustling of fabric made Tabitha think he was shrugging. "But to clarify, yes, Tabitha is beautiful, but she is also good. She will make your son a wonderful wife and be a good mother to our grandchildren."

There was a noncommittal grunt and Tabitha once again found herself frustrated that she was unable see or participate in the discussion.

"Perhaps, it is time to fetch the girl," the stranger's voice finally spoke, "and let me see for myself."

Tabitha's eyes widened and panic sprang up within her. Pressing her arms to her chest to still the tinkling of her many layers of jewelry, she tiptoed as quickly as she could back to her bedroom before she could be discovered.

She had only a moment to catch her breath before a knock came on her door. "Yes?" she asked, forcing her breathing to slow and willing her heart to stay in her chest where it belonged.

"Your father wishes you to come to him," a maid servant said from the doorway.

"Thank you, I will come now." Patting her head to double check that everything was in place, Tabitha followed the servant down to the area where her father was seated. Standing straight, she kept her chin and eyes tucked down and walked as smoothly as she could manage.

"Come, Daughter," Luram said, beckoning her toward him with a kind smile. "I will introduce you."

Tabitha swallowed hard and tried to keep her hands from trembling as she took her father's outstretched fingers and stood by his side.

"Daughter, this is Giddonah, descendant of Aminadi, who interpreted the writing on the temple walls."

Tabitha's eyes widened when she understood the importance of the man before her. Quickly schooling her features, she lifted her face and met his eyes before bending her head in reverence and hospitality.

"Welcome," Tabitha murmured. From under her lashes, she studied the older man. His skin was wrinkled and dark from days spent in the sun, while his hair stood in stark contrast, having lost its color over the years of his life. His robes were made of fine silks and fabrics in bright colors that showcased his wealth and social standing. But it was his eyes that caused Tabitha to catch her breath. They were dark, nearly black and appeared as two pools with no end. Intriguing as they were, it was the calculating intelligence that frightened her the most as they roamed over her face and frame.

Heat crept up her neck as she withstood his examination, knowing there was nothing she could do without embarrassing her father and family.

"You were indeed truthful, Friend." Giddonah finally broke the awkward silence. "She is beautiful and appears to be well behaved. I believe Amulek will be well pleased."

Amulek! Tabitha almost didn't catch the gasp that tried to break free. *This is the father to Amulek? And they wish me for his wife?*

Amulek's name was well known among the women of the city of Ammonihah, both unmarried and married alike. Although Tabitha had never seen him in person, she had heard many stories that involved him. It was said he was tall and strong and had a face that could take a woman's breath away. His family had one of the largest farms on the outskirts of the city, with thousands of livestock and workers at their command.

Why would a man who could have anyone, be interested in me? Tabitha was pulled from her mental wandering when her father cleared his throat.

"I believe we are ready for dinner now, Tabitha. Please serve us." He raised an eyebrow at her, a clear sign he was displeased she had been caught daydreaming.

"Yes, Father," she quickly replied, then walked quietly to the kitchen to start bringing out the dishes that had been prepared.

Just make it through this one meal. Tabitha encouraged herself. *Just one night.*

"Come, Daughter, we are ready," Miriam said, pulling Tabitha into the kitchen and showing her what dishes went first. "Now, stand tall and show them you have been taught the ways of running a household."

"Yes, Mother." *One night, just one night.*

Hours later, when Tabitha dropped into bed, she felt as drained mentally as she was physically. Her nerves had been tightly coiled all evening as she served food and drinks to the men. It had taken every ounce of control she had to stop the shaking in her hands at the knowledge that she was on display and even one mistake could ruin everything her father was working for. *I could not survive Father and Mother's disappointment if I failed.*

Laying on her back, Tabitha took several long, deep breaths, forcing her muscles to release and relax. Turning her head, she stared out the opening in the wall of her room, finding comfort and peace in the bright, full moon that cast its rays upon her.

With a groan, Tabitha stood up and walked toward her table, using the light shining through the window to see. Slowly, she took off the bracelets, necklaces and other adornments that were draped over her body and put them back in their places. Just as she began to strip off her robes, her door opened and her mother slipped inside.

Without a word, Miriam walked over to Tabitha and put her hand to her cheek. "You did well, Daughter." Miriam leaned in, kissed Tabitha's cheek softly then quickly left the room.

Tabitha stood in shocked silence. Although she knew her mother loved her children, Miriam had never been one to show much physical affection. To receive two shows of love in one day was unheard of and she felt as if her mother was realizing Tabitha wouldn't be around forever.

She put her fingers to her cheek. "It is as if she is saying goodbye," Tabitha murmured into the darkness.

With a small sigh and a shake of her head, Tabitha finished undressing and slipped under her blankets. Sleep claimed her tired body almost instantly, while thoughts of a strong, handsome farmer claimed her mind.

AMULEK TOOK A DEEP breath of the warm, fresh breeze blowing into his face as he stepped out of the stable and into the dying sunlight.

Despite the heat now bearing down on him, it was a relief to be away from the stifling humidity of the structure behind him.

The sound of movement caused Amulek to look over his shoulder. He nodded as his servants and farm workers began heading to their private dwellings for the evening meal. "You have done well, thank you," he said, as he slapped shoulders and nodded his thanks to those who worked under his command.

Amulek's family owned one of the biggest farms in the area. Not only did he raise large fields of corn and beans but he was in charge of thousands of sheep, goats and llamas. The work was grueling, often requiring long days and sometimes nights, but Amulek thrived in the business.

His wealth had grown exponentially since he had taken over for his father and his place in society grew increasingly important. He was often sought for his knowledge and experience in business matters and Amulek found he enjoyed the attention.

After seeing the last worker off, Amulek checked the stable door once more, ensuring no animal could break in or out, and headed to his house. Wiping the dust from his feet and sweat from his brow, he entered through the backdoor.

"Amulek!" His mother threw her arms in the air. "Every day you track dirt into my home, can you not once come in from the fields in clean clothes?" She smiled softly and cupped his cheek, undermining her scolding.

"You wish me to wash with the animals? Dress in the barn?" Amulek smiled at his mother. "Or perhaps, I should sit in the shade while my workers do all the chores and I eat grapes, hmm? That way I would not soil my clothes or your house."

"You are a good man, Amulek. Not all work as hard as you." Stepping back, she turned to the food simmering over the fire.

"Which is why not all have food to fill their bellies every night."

"And for these things, we are grateful. Now go wash, we eat soon."

Amulek grinned at the bossy tone of his mother's voice and walked down to his private room. *I am a full grown man, managing the farm in the stead of my father, and still she treats me as a boy. Do mothers ever see their children as adults?*

Once washed and changed, Amulek went back the way he came, meeting his father at the table.

"How were the fields, my son?" Giddonah slowly settled himself into the cushions on the floor, shifting his robes and limbs until he was comfortable.

"Hot," Amulek said with a grin. "The sun seeks to strip us of our strength, I think."

Giddonah nodded, thoughtfully. "At least this year it has not stripped us of our water."

"No. The rains have given us much to be thankful for," Amulek agreed with a nod. Following his father's example, Amulek seated himself on the cushions, waiting for the women to bring in the food.

"Come, Wife. We are ready," Giddonah called to Kezia.

"Yes, Husband." Amulek's mother hurried into the room, a bowl of stew in her hands. Amulek's sisters and other servants brought plates of flat bread, and platters of fruit.

After assuring that the men's plates were full, Kezia and her two daughters, Hephzibah and Mara, stood at the entrance to the room, waiting to serve more as needed.

A few moments of silence reigned as the men began to sate their hunger.

"It is good," Giddonah murmured to his wife between bites.

Dipping her head, Kezia murmured her thanks.

"Amulek, I have news for you."

Amulek ran his hand over his mouth and down his beard to clear any lingering crumbs. "Yes, Father?"

"I have found you a wife."

Amulek felt as if his very heart stopped beating at his father's announcement. He glanced at his mother, who stood stiffly, obviously aware of the impact of such news.

"A wife?"

Giddonah nodded as he continued eating, ignoring the sudden tension in the air.

"I was not informed you had taken it upon yourself to find a suitable daughter-in-law. We had an agreement that I would seek my own wife when I was established." Amulek clenched his jaw to stop from saying something more disrespectful. His father was mostly a good man, but tended to rule the house with an iron fist. When Amulek had been a young man, learning the ways of an adult, he and his father had often butted heads, causing contention and upsetting the family. Now as an adult, Amulek did his best to keep the peace, but sometimes he found it difficult. *Does he not trust me to find my own wife?*

"You have made no move to secure one for yourself and it is time you begat an heir." Giddonah scooped his stew into a piece of bread and folded it into his mouth. "You have been settled in the fields for long enough. Now it is time to settle at home."

Amulek glanced at his mother, who was standing with her chin dipped down. She looked at him from under her lashes and Amulek could read the apology in her eyes.

Taking a deep breath, Amulek did his best to release the tension in his shoulders. "Who managed to gain your approval, Father?" Amulek couldn't quite contain the sarcasm in his voice and Giddonah shot him a glare at the tone.

"Luram's daughter, Tabitha."

Amulek's eyebrows shot up.

"She is a renowned beauty and last night when I dined with her father, she served us. I believe she will make a good and dutiful wife for you." Giddonah raised an eyebrow, challenging Amulek to contradict his words.

"If she is such a beauty, why has she not already been married?"

Giddona shrugged and went back to his meal. "She is Luram's youngest. He played the sentimental father and kept her in his household longer than necessary. The union of our households would be beneficial to us both and thus he could not turn down the bargain or the dowry."

"Luram is the wool merchant we sell to, yes?" Amulek narrowed his eyes and watched his father.

Giddonah nodded. "Indeed."

"I will consider your proposal." Amulek bent back down to his meal.

"I have already arranged a contract with Luram. The wedding will be in a week's time."

Amulek's outburst overshadowed his mother's gasp. "Father, you go too far."

Giddonah clenched his fist and banged it on the table. "It is a father's right to approve the marriage of his children." His face grew red and his voice louder as he continued. "You will marry her in a week and fulfill the bargain that has been signed. Our family honor will not be sacrificed simply for your convenience."

Amulek glared back at his father, his chest heaving in unfulfilled anger. After a moment, his eyes once again darted to the back of the room, taking in the way his sisters shrank into themselves and the pleading look in his mother's eyes. Amulek's heart dropped. *If I don't accept this, I hurt my mother and sisters.* He sighed. *Maybe, it will be alright. Maybe I will be able to get along with her. Surely, father would not choose a woman who would be an embarrassment. No,* he thought grimly. *His pride is too great for that.* Swallowing his own pride, Amulek forced a stiff nod. "One week," he said through clenched teeth.

Although she made no audible noise, Amulek could see the relief pass over his mother's face and the tightness drain from her shoulders. Kezia sent him a small smile of gratitude before attending to her husband's needs.

At least one of us has found peace with the situation.

Later that evening, as the household was preparing for bed, Amulek found himself standing at a window, staring into the night sky; his hands clasped behind his back.

"Amulek?" a soft, feminine voice called from the darkness behind him.

"Hephzibah?" Amulek asked as he turned. "What are you doing awake? Mother sent you and Mara to bed long ago."

His sister bit her lip and looked down at her bare feet, then back up. "I know, but I wished to tell you something."

Amulek took a moment to study his sister in the moonlight. Very soon she would be considered a woman and leave his house as she found the man she was to marry. *Or the one father wishes her to marry,* he thought bitterly. Her dark hair hung to her waist and her features were beginning to mature into that of a beautiful, young lady. There were several years between him and his sisters. His mother had lost two children between the siblings and needless to say, the two girls had brought Kezia great joy after so much loss.

"What did you need, Sister?" Amulek spoke softly, so as not to awaken the household.

"I have seen, Tabitha." Hephzibah walked closer and rested her small hand on Amulek's arm.

"My Tabitha? Luram's daughter?"

Hephzibah nodded. Grasping her robe, she pulled it tight about her figure, hugging herself. "She is indeed a great beauty, but more importantly... she is kind. I often see her gathering water at the fountain. She always has a smile for those around her and I have seen her help the older women carry their loads."

For the first time since his father's announcement, Amulek felt a small measure of hope. "You believe she will be a good wife?"

Hephzibah shrugged. "I do not know of her skills as a wife, but I believe she will be an agreeable companion. Truly, I do not know how father managed to convince Luram to let her go. The rumor in the village is that many have tried to bargain with him, but he has always turned them down."

"I wonder what changed his mind," Amulek murmured, turning back to the window.

"Maybe none of the other men had as much to offer as Father," his sister suggested.

Amulek nodded. "Thank you," he said over his shoulder. "You have eased my mind this night."

"Goodnight, Brother," came her soft reply.

"Goodnight."

CHAPTER 2

Despite the stale, unrelenting heat from the afternoon sun and the many bodies crammed into her room, Tabitha felt shaky and cold all over. Her teeth chattered, and she felt moist as sweat drenched her underclothes.

Miriam tsked her tongue. "Daughter, you will ruin our efforts if you do not gain control of yourself."

"Sorry, Mother," Tabitha whispered. Her chest felt tight and she could hardly breath. The headdress of feathers and beads that sat on her crown felt as if it would crush her into the floor.

Tabitha had spent the last several hours letting the women prepare her for her wedding day, but despite the comfort of those she loved being close to her, Tabitha felt scared and alone.

What if he doesn't like what he sees? What if his eyes are as cold as his father's? What if I cannot like him? What if I am a disappointment?

Her thoughts were brought back to the present when Miriam and the other women stepped back to view their handiwork. Tabitha knew that today of all days, she should feel beautiful and desired, but it was difficult when she was so nervous about the marriage.

Earlier she had been bathed in fresh, cool water, then rubbed from head to toe in scented oils. Her hair had been brushed until it was dry and gleaming then smoothed with yet more oils. Layer upon layer of silks and fine fabrics had been draped on her body, meant to show her status and wealth. A thin veil covered most of her face, leaving only her eyes clearly visible. Her eyes were rimmed in black and a servant had put a thick cream on her lips to moisten and highlight them. Chains and trinkets of gold had then been wound around every limb, from her ankles to her head. Every movement caused a tinkling sound that was beginning to bother Tabitha's already raw nerves.

Miriam put her clasped fingers to her lips and blinked back tears. "It is well," she whispered, her voice thick with emotion and barely audible.

Tabitha blinked rapidly to hold back her own tears and nodded to her mother.

"Come, it is time." Miriam put out one hand and walked through the door, Tabitha following in her wake.

Once in the gathering room, Tabitha's eyes found her father's.

"My beautiful daughter," he murmured with a smile before crossing the room with his hands outstretched. He wrapped his arms around Tabitha and held her for a few moments. "You bring much good to this family," he whispered in her ear. Putting his hands on her shoulders, he leaned back to look her in the eye.

"No tears, dear daughter." He chuckled and wiped the stray droplets that had trickled down her smooth cheek. "You will ruin all the hard work your mother has put into your appearance."

Tabitha tried to smile, but it felt stiff and strained. She wanted nothing more than to stay in her father's firm and safe embrace. An embrace that spoke of home and comfort. She knew marriage was a good thing and that building her own family was something to be desired, but fear of the unknown was overpowering every other rational thought.

A knock on the door caused Tabitha to gasp and step back.

Luram smiled and patted her shoulder. "Your betrothed has arrived. Let us not keep him waiting." Walking swiftly to the door, Lumar opened it wide. "Welcome, Bridegroom Amulek."

"I have come to collect my bride," a deep, commanding voice said from the opening.

Tabitha felt her hand flutter up to her neck. The tone of his voice was invigorating and had a quality in it that sent the butterflies in her stomach into an even greater tizzy.

"Come, Daughter. Meet your Groom." Lumar had stepped back and waved a hand at Tabitha.

With a stuttered breath, she reached out and took her father's hand, allowing him to pull her into the light of the door.

She kept her head and eyes down as she was presented to Amulek, but when his large, tanned hand entered her vision, beckoning to her, she could no longer hold herself back. Slowly, she let her eyes drift upward until she met his gaze.

Tabitha took in a quick breath through her nose as she saw her soon to be husband. He stood tall and proud. His broad shoulders nearly filled the doorway. His face was more than pleasant, with a strong jaw and straight nose. His beard was neatly trimmed close to his skin. His lips were slightly turned up in a small, reassuring smile. But it was his eyes that caught her attention. They were dark, like his father's but unlike the calculating coldness she had seen last week, Amulek's eyes were kind but slightly wary.

Is he nervous as well? The idea that he might have feelings similar to her own anxieties gave Tabitha a measure of hope.

Holding his gaze, she took her hand from her father's and slipped it into Amulek's calloused palm. A light, tingle of warmth ran up her arm as they touched, creating an unexpected, soothing balm to her nerves.

"Are you ready, my Betrothed?" Amulek's voice was soft as he studied her.

"Yes, my Bridegroom. I am yours to take," Tabitha recited the lines only loud enough for him to hear.

He smiled again, creasing the corners of his eyes, and nodded. "Then come." Keeping a hold of her hand, he turned and led the procession to the building where the feast and ceremony were to be held.

AMULEK COULDN'T KEEP his gaze from straying to the beautiful woman at his side as they walked. *She is more than I could have asked for.*

Her beauty had nearly struck him speechless when she lifted her face to look at him.

Like most of the women in the city, her hair was dark and long. What he could see of it under her headdress, gleamed in the light of the evening sun, appearing soft and silky. Its color was so dark it appeared black. The color matched the lashes that had fanned her cheeks when she stared at the ground. Long and thick, they framed the most exquisite eyes he had ever seen. Unlike most of the women in the village, her eyes were not varying shades of brown. Instead, they were a mix of brown and green, with the green being dominate. The light color stood out in startling contrast to the silks and linens showcasing her face.

Her other features had proved to be just as appealing. Her nose was small and straight and the skin that was visible was light, soft and unmarred.

Truly, Father was right. She is a rare beauty.

The longer he stared at her, the warmer the sensation in his chest became. He cleared his throat, knowing the feeling had nothing to do with the heat of the evening sun bearing down on him.

Slowly, they padded through the dusty, cobbled streets until they approached a large building near the center of the city. The massive crowd that had followed them, now surged forward, filling the space and awaiting the engaged couple.

Amulek paused for a moment, firming his resolve to move forward with this momentous occasion that would affect the rest of his life. His chest felt tight and not for the first time, he had to fight down a feeling of resentment at his father. *No more,* he scolded himself. *Today should be a happy occasion.*

A light squeeze on his hand caught his attention. Looking down, he found Tabitha's eyes upon him. Their unusual color was especially vivid in the fading light, but more importantly, Amulek found himself intrigued that her eyes did not speak of haughtiness or entitlement. They appeared soft and kind. *She is very much how Hephzibah described.*

Although Tabitha's lips were covered by a veil, a small wrinkling at the edge of her eyes let Amulek know she was smiling at him. Nodding, he led the way through the crowd where their families had assembled.

Hours later, Amulek couldn't eat another bite. He shifted on his pillow and leaned back away from the table. Hundreds of people swarmed the area, eating, dancing and making merry. Wine flowed freely, causing the noise level to rise as each hour passed.

He glanced at Tabitha, who sat quietly with wide eyes at the celebration surrounding them. She had hardly eaten a bite and Amulek worried she would become hungry later.

The ceremony of their joining had been swift and without complication. Each had recited the lines necessary to fulfill the bond, and they had been declared man and wife. When he had taken Tabitha's hand, she had been trembling slightly, and he felt a measure of sympathy for her.

She is leaving all she knows and trusting herself to a man who is a complete stranger to her. That situation would terrify even the strongest of individuals.

He leaned down until he was right next to her ear. "Are you all right, Wife?"

Her stunning eyes preceded her face as she turned to look at him. Amulek moved his head back only slightly, staying close. *Just so I can hear her reply,* he told himself.

"I am well, thank you," she murmured. She glanced down at his empty plate. "May I serve you something? Are you yet hungry?"

Amulek smiled. "No, thank you. I have filled myself more than I should. You might have to have me carried home if I consume more."

An amused smile pulled at Tabitha's mouth; easing the tension in her face. Closing her eyes, she put her chin down and laughed lightly before looking back up. "That would probably not be the best start to our life together, would it?"

"Indeed, not." Amulek let his eyes wander over her. Her veil had been removed for the meal and he was finally able to see the rest of her face.

Her high cheekbones and full lips were just as he imagined them. He found himself fascinated at the blush that crept up her cheeks at his perusal. Reaching out, he traced one finger along her jawline and up around her pink cheek. "You are very beautiful, Tabitha. However, you have probably been told that your whole life."

Tabitha's eyes dropped, and she chewed her lip, obviously uncomfortable with his comment. Amulek frowned, put a finger under her chin and raised her face back up.

"What is wrong?"

Tabitha gave a small shake of her head. "I am not used to such words, Husband. I find myself no more beautiful than the other women in the city. Saying such things will only serve to give me a big head."

Amulek grinned and went back to caressing her face with his finger. He couldn't seem to stop touching her soft, fair skin. "I speak only the truth, dear one. And if it proves to make your head large, we will simply build bigger entrances to our home."

Her eyes widened with surprise, then softened into a grateful look. "Thank you for your kindness. I will admit that I find you most pleasing to look at, as well." Her eyes fell away from his at her confession in a shy gesture.

"Ah, are women not taught to say such things to their husbands?" He grinned. "Flatter him endlessly so he will please her and buy her trinkets and such?"

Tabitha's eyes widened and her mouth dropped open. "No! I was not, I mean I did not wish to-" She stopped speaking as Amulek chuckled at her panic.

"Calm yourself, Wife. I was merely teasing." He tucked a stray hair behind her ear, then fingered the long length of it. *It is just as silky as it appears.* "It is obvious you are shy and ill at ease. I was simply trying to bring another smile to your lovely face."

Tabitha's shoulders dropped and she let out a long breath. "I apologize that my nerves are so easily seen. I knew not what to expect this afternoon. Although I have heard your name in the city, I knew very little about you. I was unaware that my father was planning to broker a contract between our families until it was already happening." She looked into his eyes and smiled softly. "I suppose I am still adjusting. I beg your patience in this."

Amulek nodded thoughtfully. "My father also surprised me with the idea. At first, I was upset that I was not allowed to choose for myself. But after seeing you and speaking with you, I believe we will have a good marriage, Tabitha."

She hesitantly raised her hand and gently cupped his cheek. "I will do my best to make you a good wife," she said so softly he could barely hear her over the pounding of his heart.

"And I will do the same." He turned his head and kissed her palm, before taking it in his own. Facing back towards the room, Amulek put his arm around Tabitha's shoulders and tucked her into his side "Come, let us watch the dancing for a little while."

When she relaxed into his hold, even cuddling a little closer, Amulek felt his heart warm. *All will be well.*

Several hours later, Amulek could feel Tabitha's head becoming heavy on his shoulder. Glancing down, he saw her eyelids blinking rapidly as if she was forcing herself to stay awake.

He smiled and shifted so she sat up. "Are you ready to leave so soon?"

Tabitha smiled sleepily. "I fear I am not used to late nights."

Amulek nodded and ran a knuckle down her cheek. "As a farmer's wife, that will not change. I often rise before the sun."

Tabitha smiled. "I will do my best to follow your example."

Amulek continued to find himself entranced by her beauty and sweetness. Unable to stop himself, he cupped her chin and leaned down until their lips were almost touching. "Thank you, Tabitha," he breathed. "I find my fears of starting married life washing away with every word you speak." Lightly, so as not to scare her, he kissed her lips and pulled back.

Tabitha's eyes fluttered closed, and she sighed as he pulled away. With a smile, he leaned back in and held onto her longer.

"Thank you, Amulek," she whispered as he straightened. "I, too, was fearful, but you have been more than I could have hoped for."

Amulek smiled wide and stood up. Offering his hand down, he pulled her up to meet him. "Come, Wife. Our time here is done."

CHAPTER 3

As the first streams of warm sunlight trickled through the bedroom window, Amulek found himself rising into gradual awareness. Blinking several times, he let the memories of his marriage wash over him before glancing at Tabitha's dark head lying next to him.

Despite his original reservations, Hephzibah's knowledge had proved to be true. His wife was gentle and beautiful, the kind of woman he would have picked for himself if given the choice.

The temperature in the room began to spike as the sun continued to rise and Amulek held in a groan. *The fields and flocks will not wait.* Carefully, he slipped out of bed, doing his best not to disturb his sleeping wife, and dressed for the day's work.

After quietly closing his door, he made his way to the kitchen to eat before leaving to take care of the herds. He was surprised to find his mother there, helping prepare breakfast.

"I assumed you would sleep in after such a late night," Amulek said as he kissed her wrinkled cheek.

Kezia smiled and patted his jaw. "I did not wish that your beautiful bride would wake up and have no one to greet her." She glanced behind Amulek, then back. "Is she still sleeping?"

"Yes. I arose quietly and slipped out to allow her more time for rest."

Kezia smiled and went back to her work.

"Mother," Amulek hesitated in the doorway.

Kezia turned and looked at him with an expectant expression.

"She appears to be a shy and quiet woman. Please be gentle with her today."

His mother's face softened. "I saw the two of you last night. It is obvious you were pleased with her. I promise I will love her as I do my own daughters."

Amulek nodded with a grateful smile, grabbed a piece of fruit and ducked out the doorway to the fields.

TABITHA STRETCHED AS the warm sunlight caressed her face. Distant shouts from outside her window caused her to open her eyes. The sun was higher than she expected and she quickly looked over to the empty side of the bed.

"What kind of wife will he think I am when I sleep away the day?" Quickly, she moved from the blankets over to the wash stand. Taking a few moments to cleanse and refresh herself, she hurriedly dressed and slipped out the door.

The smell of warm breads and meats led her down the hallway toward the cooking area. Peeking around the corner, she saw several women working over fires and at tables.

Amulek's mother glanced up at Tabitha's entrance and gasped. "Daughter!" With a wide smile, Kezia wrapped a stunned Tabitha in a welcoming hug.

Slowly, Tabitha's tension melted at the motherly gesture and she wrapped her arms around her new mother, returning the embrace.

Standing back, Kezia kept her hands on Tabitha's shoulders and looked her over. "You look beautiful this morning, Daughter. Did my son treat you well?"

Tabitha's eyes widened and her jaw grew slack. She felt her cheeks begin to burn as if they would cause a fire, but no words came out of her mouth.

Kezia chuckled and patted Tabitha's cheek. "That look says it all. Come. Do not be nervous, you are a woman now and my daughter. All is as it should be." Leading Tabitha by the hand, Kezia brought her to the table and seated her in front of a plate filled with fruit and bread.

"Eat." Kezia said with a kind smile. "The rest of the household is up and about and has had their share."

"I fear I overslept this morning. Please, forgive me," Tabitha tucked her chin, worried she had caused a grievous error in her laziness.

Once again, Kezia reached out. Putting a finger under Tabitha's chin, she brought her face up. "Every woman deserves a rest after her marriage night. There is nothing to forgive." Kezia chuckled as she walked back toward her work in the kitchen. "Not to mention, my son begged a promise that we would let you rest as long as you desired today." She glanced at Tabitha over her shoulder. "He wished you to have everything you needed, including sleep."

Tabitha's cheeks heated yet again and this time when she ducked her chin, it was to hide the smile that wanted to break across her face. *Truly, my husband is a kind man to be so concerned for my welfare.*

After Tabitha had filled her hungry belly, she picked up her plate and delivered it to the area to wash dishes. "What would you have me do, Mother?" she quietly asked Kezia.

Kezia smiled. "Ah, Daughter, you are truly as kind and gentle as Amulek said. Are you up to washing today?"

"Of course."

Kezia nodded her approval. "Take Hephzibah and Mara with you. They are still learning to ways of womanhood and your influence will be very valuable."

"I will do my best." Tabitha returned to her room to gather the bed linens before heading outside for the baskets of soiled clothing.

"Hello," a young, feminine voice greeted her.

Tabitha spun around to see two young girls, one on the cusp of womanhood standing by the entrance to the house. "Hello, I am Tabitha. Wife of Amulek." *This must be Amulek's sisters.* Anxiety raced through

Tabitha along with a sudden need to make a good impression. *Amulek has been so kind, I do not wish to upset any of his family.*

"I am Hephzibah. Daughter of Giddonah and sister to Amulek," the oldest stated. "And this is my sister Mara."

Tabitha smiled shyly. "Good morning, sisters. It is easy to see that you take after your mother. You are both very beautiful."

Mara put her hand over her mouth to hold in a giggle and Tabitha sighed in relief.

Hephzibah smiled at her younger sister before looking back at Tabitha. "It is also easy to see why Father chose you for our brother. You are truly beautiful, but your eyes are very unusual. I have never seen their like."

Tabitha bit her bottom lip. Her light-colored eyes had been a constant source of trial for her. Girls her age often made fun of them, while men watched her from afar as if she were a specimen to be examined.

"It is no wonder our brother was so taken with you," Mara squeaked out before giggling again.

Tabitha smiled. *They mean no harm.* "You flatter me, dear sisters. I can tell we will truly get along well. Now come, your mother has asked we wash the soiled clothes. If we hurry, we can finish before the midday sun melts us to a puddle."

Both girls smiled wide, nodded, and gathered baskets in their arms before following Tabitha to the well.

AMULEK SIGHED AND WIPED his sticky brow as he walked toward the house. Long shadows covered the dusty ground as the sun sank lower into the horizon. He paused a moment and looked over his shoulder at the beauty of the landscape.

Putting his hands on his hips, he closed his eyes, soaking in the last rays of light and pulling a deep breath in through his nose. Dust, sweat, animals and fresh, open fields fought for dominance in the scent laden air. *It is good.* With a content nod, Amulek turned back to the house and continued his journey.

Eagerness hastened his footsteps as he thought of his wife waiting for him. *I wonder how her day went. Is she comfortable here? Will she find peace amongst my kindred?*

He thought of her unusual green eyes. *They are stunning.* "I suspect Father felt she would elevate our status with her beauty." He grimaced for a moment. Regardless of his father's purpose, Amulek was grateful for the woman who had been given to him. She was kind and humble in a way that was unusual in their city. Many of their thriving city were followers of the teachings of Nehor and prescribed to the thinking of popularity and excess as a way of life.

Amulek focused on the ground and frowned as he walked. *Seeking after status and wealth are not where our ambitions should lie and I am grateful that Tabitha seems to be of the same mind.*

Amulek's mind brushed over the teachings of his ancestors. He came from a line of believers, some of whom had performed miracles in the name of the Lord. But as time passed, the teachings had fallen out of favor, even though King Mosiah and the people of his city still believed them.

A sharp prick hit Amulek in the chest and he absently rubbed his hand over the spot. Lately, he had been curious about the teachings his family had left behind, but was unable bring himself to throw aside all he had to embrace them.

With a sharp shake of his head, Amulek once again pushed the musings away. Looking up, he was only a few feet from the house and he smiled when he caught a whiff of the meat cooking over the fire.

Kezia, his mother looked up at his entrance. "Welcome home, my son. How were the flocks and fields today?"

"Same as always, Mother." He gave her his customary kiss on the cheek. "And where is my beautiful wife? Is she all right?" His brows furrowed in concern. He had thought she would be helping with the evening meal.

Kezia smiled. "She is well. All was in hand here, so she chose to tend to the needs of your father. She is sitting at his feet, listening to his stories the rest of us have heard too many times."

Amulek's chest warmed from Tabitha's kindness. "She will make a friend for life if she continues to spoil him."

Kezia nodded her head as she bent over her work. "Indeed."

Amulek took a few steps toward the sitting room.

"Amulek, if you wish your wife to welcome you to her arms, you might wish to wash the filth from yourself first." Kezia put her hands on her hips and narrowed her eyes.

Amulek's eyebrows shot up. "Do you mean to say I do not smell sweet, Mother? I carry the scent of the sheep and the corn fields on my shoulders. Is that not fresh and welcoming?"

Kezia tilted her head and shrugged. "I do not believe she planned to marry a wooly lamb. The scent of her husband is surely more enticing."

Amulek chuckled, stepped back and gave her another quick kiss. "I will do as you suggest, Mother. Thank you." Striding quickly to his room, he changed his outer work tunic and washed himself at the basin of water in his room. "Surely now, she will now welcome me," he murmured with a grin.

Shoulders straight and chin up, he walked to find his wife and father. He found them exactly as his mother had stated. Giddonah sat in his chair, resting against the pillows and cushions in a languid manner. One of his hands swung through the air, as he relayed a story from his youth.

Tabitha sat at his feet, cloth and needle resting forgotten in her lap as she listened to her father-in-law speak.

"Is his story so interesting you have forgotten the mending, dear wife?" Amulek teased from the corner of the room.

With a light gasp, Tabitha spun on her hip to see him. A pleased smile crept across her face and she ducked her chin. "Good evening, Husband."

"Did I not tell you she would make a good wife?" Giddonah smiled triumphantly before standing. "She knows her place well and was worth the large dowry." He nodded at Tabitha's down-turned head and walked toward the dining area.

Amulek clenched his jaw to keep from speaking. He could see that Tabitha's smile had drooped at his father's words.

Determined to make Tabitha smile once more, Amulek crossed the floor and crouched down next to her. He lifted her chin with his knuckle until she looked him in the eye. "Good evening, Wife." Slowly, he leaned in for short kiss.

When he pulled back, Tabitha's eyes stayed closed for a few moments before she fluttered them open. The light green depths spoke of being pleased with his greeting. He grinned and rubbed his knuckle down her cheek. "And how did you spend your day? Hmm? Surely you did not sit and listen to my father's tales for so many hours?"

Tabitha laughed lightly and Amulek rejoiced in the sound.

"Indeed, not. I'm afraid I nearly slept the morning away, but your mother was gracious enough to feed me when I finally awoke."

Amulek took Tabitha's hand and stood, pulling her with him. After settling her and himself on a bench, he held both of her hands in his lap. "I asked Mother to let you rest. Yesterday was overwhelming for both of us."

"And yet, you rose with the sun," Tabitha said with a smile.

Amulek pursed his lips and nodded; his head down as he stared at their entwined hands. "Too many years of doing so to quit now that I am a married man."

Tabitha squeezed his fingers to get his attention. "I am grateful for such a dedicated husband."

Time seemed to slow as they smiled at each other, but Amulek broke the spell with another question. "After you ate, did you then spend the day at my father's feet?" Amulek smiled to let her know he was teasing. "Surely, even he does not have enough stories to keep you entertained that long."

"No." Tabitha gave a breathy laugh. "I helped with washing the fabrics and clothes today. Your sisters, Hephzibah and Mara went with me to the well."

"Ah. You have met the two troublemakers of the family. And how did you fair in their presence?"

Tabitha gave a light push on his hands. "They were angels. I shall enjoy having them as sisters." She raised an eyebrow at Amulek. "I am starting to think I am married to the troublemaker, as you are proving to be one who teases often."

Amulek laughed. "Yes, that is probably true. I prefer lightness and laughter after a long day of work."

"Another thing for which I am grateful. I did not know what to-" Tabitha caught herself and bit her lip; her eyes darting away from him.

Amulek took hold of her chin and brought her back to face him. "It is all right. I too, was unsure what to expect in the woman I was given to marry. But you are proving to be sweet and gentle, just as I would have hoped. Not to mention more beautiful than I would have dreamed. I am finding myself honored to be your husband." His eyes roved over her face and his fingers slid along the underside of her jaw.

WHAT IS THIS FEELING? Tabitha felt warm and tingly all over as Amulek's strong fingers slid over her skin. She knew she needed to respond to his kind words, but her tongue felt dry and rough and she was having trouble concentrating.

"I had heard a great deal about you in the city. You have a reputation among the men as a wealthy and intelligent businessman. Yet the women gossip about your looks with stars in their eyes," she finally forced out.

Amulek huffed a laugh and smiled.

"I find both rumors to be true, yet most importantly, I have found you are also generous and kind, qualities I had always hoped to find. I too, am honored to be married to one such as you." Tabitha's heart felt like it would beat out of her chest. Speaking her mind, especially to someone she barely knew was a difficult thing for her. She had always been quiet and observant, rather than talkative and social.

"Thank you, Wife. Your words mean much to me." Amulek leaned in and captured her lips in a soft, lingering kiss.

Tabitha let out an involuntary sigh when he pulled away and she immediately felt embarrassed at her own reaction. Pulling back, she hid behind her scarf to cover the blush creeping up her neck, but Amulek only chuckled and stood.

"Come, let us join the evening meal before your husband wastes away from hunger." He pulled Tabitha to stand beside him and led her to the dining area with a hand on her lower back.

Amulek's teasing manner had helped Tabitha's embarrassment begin to recede until they arrived at the table where four sets of eyes watched their every move.

His two sisters were smiling and giggling, while Kezia looked pleased at her and Amulek. However, Giddonah, although not angry, always seemed to be calculating and assessing those around him and it sent a slight chill down Tabitha's spine.

She had spent time at his feet today, listening to his tales of youth and mischief in an effort to get to know him. However, even after their time together, she couldn't shake the feeling that Giddonah was constantly measuring her actions. *His body may be old, but his mind is truly as sharp as any young man.*

"Excuse our late entrance, Father. Tabitha and I are still getting to know each other." Amulek's easy manner calmed Tabitha's nerves as he settled on the pillows and cushions at the table.

"You are newly married," Giddonah grunted. "The excitement will fade with time and then will no longer interrupt our household." He picked up his beans with a piece of bread and took a bite.

Tabitha's ever present blush once again heated her cheeks. *I should not have kept Amulek from his family.* She saw Amulek's jaw clench before he forced it to relax.

"Forgive us for beginning without you," Kezia whispered with a soft smile. "We wished to allow you time together."

Tabitha relaxed a little and smiled in gratitude while Amulek spoke. "All is well, Mother. But now I must fill my stomach or I will surely perish." He grinned as he reached for his plate.

Giddonah chuckled while his wife tsked her tongue.

Tabitha felt the last of her tension drain out of her shoulders.

The rest of the meal was quiet as the women waited at the edge of the room for the men to finish eating. Tabitha could not seem to keep her gaze from straying to her husband. Each time, she glanced up, finding his gaze upon her and her cheeks would burn with heat. *Soon I will burn to ashes if I continued to react this way.*

At last the eating dwindled, Tabitha approached Amulek. "Is there anything more I can get you, Husband?"

Mischief twinkled in his eyes as he smiled at her. "I am full, thank you. But I would like to speak to you after you have finished eating."

"Of course," she murmured. *Did I do something wrong?*

Once the men had retired to a small sitting room, Tabitha and the other women quickly ate their suppers. As she stood to help clean up, Kezia stopped her. "Go, Daughter. Your husband waits."

Tabitha hesitated, then nodded and walked to where Amulek was conversing with his father. She thought she might burst into flame from the heat of embarrassment as Amulek rose to take her hand and let him lead her down the hall to the main sitting area. She could hear Mara giggle behind them, only to be shushed by a deep, gruff voice.

Amulek let go of her hand and Tabitha stood against the wall with her arms wrapped around her middle.

"I apologize, Wife." Amulek turned to her and ran a knuckle down her cheek. "It would appear that I embarrassed you this evening."

"It is of no consequence," she said softly. "It is a wife's duty to follow her husband. I apologize if I offended you this evening."

Amulek frowned. "I do not wish for you to follow me like a blind lamb, Tabitha. I wish for our marriage to be a partnership. For you to follow because you wish to, not because you are ordered to."

Hope shot straight through Tabitha. Despite the societal norms, she had always hoped for a marriage based in love and Amulek seemed to be telling her that he also sought more than convention dictated.

As Tabitha's thoughts swirled, Amulek stepped closer. "I fear my father's opinions have led you to believe that I wish for a subservient woman who will never go against my judgement." He pushed a wisp of hair behind her ear and let his finger linger on her cheek.

Tabitha felt as if she couldn't breathe. Every muscle in her body had seized up at his touch, awaiting his next words.

"I wish for us to get along, but I wish for a help-meet most of all. I want to hear your thoughts and opinions and wish to share my own." He wrapped both hands around her back and pulled her into his chest. "I wish for you to tell me if I am acting out of turn." He nuzzled his face into her hair. "I do not desire for our children to fear any time I am challenged."

Tabitha felt tears pricking the back of her eyes as she listened to his sweet words. Her arms were wrapped around his torso and she clung tightly to him. An overwhelming sense of gratefulness rushed through her at the generosity of the man in her arms.

Pulling back slightly, Amulek looked down into her face. "Have you nothing to say, Tabitha?"

She blinked rapidly, attempting to keep the tears at bay. "Thank you, Amulek. Your words mean more than I can say. I was afraid when I was being sent to marry a stranger that I would never find joy and happiness." She reached up and ran her fingers along his beard. "You are proving to be what I dreamed but dare not hope for."

Amulek smiled. "We will learn together, yes?"

Tabitha smiled and nodded, then leaned closer as her husband closed the distance between them.

CHAPTER 4

Tabitha wrung her hands together as she waited for Amulek to arrive from the fields for the evening meal. She had been restless the past couple of days but had been working hard not to show her nerves.

Life had fallen into a monotonous but pleasant routine in Amulek's household. In the last couple of months, Tabitha had slid easily into her role as wife and Kezia had begun to hand over more of the household duties into Tabitha's capable hands.

Although there were still occasional tense moments with Giddonah, for the most part, life ran smoothly.

But today, Tabitha was anxious for her husband to arrive.

"Looking at the door will not bring my son any faster." Kezia chuckled as she finished the platter of fruit she had been working on.

"I am sorry, Mother." Tabitha's cheeks turned pink. "I find myself particularly excited for my husband's return this evening."

Kezia nodded. "And I look forward to the announcement that will bring as well."

Tabitha's head jerked toward her mother-in-law.

Kezia smiled. "From one woman to another, your secret is safe with me."

Tabitha walked over and embraced the woman who had taken her under her wing. Kezia's kindness and acceptance had made a world of difference in helping Tabitha find her place in the family.

"Thank you," Tabitha whispered as a stray tear trickled down her cheek.

"Thank *you*," Kezia sniffed in return.

"Although I am grateful that my two favorite women enjoy each other's company, I am concerned to find the household in tears." Amulek's voice rang from the doorway and the two women jumped apart.

"Amulek!" Kezia put her hand over her heart. "Have you no respect for an old woman's nerves?"

Her scolding tone relieved Amulek's face of the worry it held. "Old woman? I see no old woman before me." He kissed his mother's cheek. "You are as young as the day you married father."

"Oh," Kezia shooed him away with her hands, but a wide smile sat on her face. "Do not let your lies become a habit, Son. It does not become you." Kezia winked at Tabitha then bent back to her work.

"What has you in tears this evening, hmm?" Amulek cupped Tabitha's face and wiped a stray drip at the corner of her eye.

Tabitha swallowed and forced a smile. "I am simply grateful to have such a wonderful family."

Amulek narrowed his eyes. "Spinning the truth must be a family problem."

Tabitha's smile grew more genuine. "We will talk later, Husband."

Amulek nodded. "I will wash up before we eat." Leaving Tabitha with a quick peck on the lips, he strode down the hall to their private chambers.

Once dinner was over, Tabitha quickly went through her chores of helping clear the food and mess while Amulek rested and spoke with his father. When things were done, she walked to the gathering room entrance and leaned against the doorway.

"Tabitha." Amulek looked up and smiled. "Come." He held out his hand and Tabitha eagerly walked over to join him.

"Husband," Kezia called softly from the doorway. "Shall we retire?"

Giddonah narrowed his eyes at his wife then glanced at Amulek and Tabitha and back before nodding. "Send the girls to bed and I shall join you," Giddonah spoke as he rose from his seat.

Once they were alone, Amulek pulled Tabitha from her cushion and tugged her into his lap. "Mmm…" He hummed into Tabitha's neck. "You smell sweet. Nothing like the llamas I tend to each day."

Tabitha giggled and ran her fingers through Amulek's shoulder length hair. "I should hope not! What man desires a wife who smells like an animal?"

Amulek shrugged playfully. "Certainly not I. I much prefer to keep my wife in fine clothes and smelling of flowers." He brushed her hair off her shoulder.

"And I am grateful for all you provide," Tabitha said in sincerity. "And now I have something for you in return."

Amulek pulled his head back and smiled. "You wish to give me a gift?"

Tabitha smiled. "Yes, but I do not have it ready for you, you will need to be patient."

Amulek's frowned in confusion. "You have a gift but you do not have it?"

Tabitha laughed and put her hands on either side of his face. "The gift is growing and will be here sometime next spring."

Amulek's eyes widened and his gaze dropped to her stomach. Slowly, he reached a hand out and rested his large hand on her abdomen. "You are sure?"

"Yes, my dear husband." Tabitha's heart dropped when he didn't speak more. "Are you not happy? I thought-" She cut herself off and bit her lips between her teeth. "I'm sorry. I shouldn't have bothered you." Bolting off of his lap, Tabitha ran to their bedroom.

Once inside, she hurried to the window, taking in large breaths of night air to clear the dizzy spell she felt from her run. She knew she wouldn't have privacy for long and she was desperately trying to pull herself back together before Amulek arrived.

"Tabitha," his deep voice rang from the doorway.

Tabitha's stomach churned. *I shouldn't have run away from him. A good wife wouldn't do that.* "I am sorry," she murmured, turning around with her head down. "I will not bother you again."

AMULEK FELT AS IF HE'D been hit in the chest with a rock. He had been so stunned at Tabitha's news that he had frozen when he realized what she was telling him. And in doing so, he had hurt her.

"Tabitha," he breathed in sorrow. Shutting the door behind him, he swiftly crossed the room and gathered her into his arms.

This beautiful woman who had been forced upon him had become one of the most important parts of his life. He loved coming home in the evenings and listening to her talk about her day. Her smile cured a multitude of ills and her laughter brought joy to his heart.

And now she was cuddled into his chest, crying because he had been so surprised at her announcement.

"Dear, sweet, Tabitha," he said soothingly. He put his hands on her cheeks and lifted her tear-stained face to look at him. "Forgive me. Your words caught me by surprise."

Tabitha nodded and a trembling smile crossed her face. "I apologize. I should not have-"

"No." Amulek interrupted her with a quick kiss. "I did not mean to hurt you, I was simply surprised." He smiled. "Is there any greater news for a man than to hear that his wife will bear him a son?"

He could see the sorrow drain from Tabitha's face and her smile became more genuine. "And how will you feel if it is a daughter, instead?".

Amulek kissed the top of her head. "Then I will be doubly blessed. For she will be as beautiful as her mother, and who could not help but love having two such women in their lives?"

Tabitha looked up with a shocked face. "You love me?"

Amulek's eyebrows furrowed. "Of course. Have you doubted?"

Tabitha's cheeks turned pink, and she chewed on her lip. Her eyes dropped to his chest as she spoke. "You have been nothing but kind and generous since we wed, but I know you did not agree with your father forcing you to marry. I did not allow myself to hope you would love me. I was simply grateful for your kindness."

Amulek's heart sped up as she spoke. *Does she not return my feelings, then? Can she not reconcile herself to love the man chosen for her?*

Resting her small hands on his chest, Tabitha looked up into Amulek's eyes and smiled. "I love you, too."

Joy soared through him. "Has ever a man been more blessed? To have the love of his woman and a child on the way, truly I could not ask for more." Leaning down he kissed his wife.

CHAPTER 5

"Amulek! You must come quick!"

Amulek dropped the bundle of corn he had been carrying and jerked toward the person calling his name. "Mara? What is it?" He ran to meet his frantic sister.

"It is Tabitha," Mara gasped. "Mother said you must come."

Amulek's heart seemed to stop. "Tabitha," he breathed. Without waiting for his sister, he bolted out of the field and ran as fast as he could for the house.

Bursting through the doorway, he began yelling her name. "Tabitha! Tabitha!"

The servants were scurrying through the home and all of them jumped at his sudden entrance.

"Where is she?" he shouted, pushing his way further into the home. "Tabitha!"

"Amulek!" Kezia came running down the hallway from Amulek's private chambers.

"Mother!" He closed the distance between them and grabbed her by the shoulders. "What has happened? Where is Tabitha?" He noted the tears streaking down his mother's face and his heart plummeted even more.

"She is in the small building on the edge of the property, Son. She-"

Amulek didn't stay to hear what she had to say. As soon as he knew where she was, he ran to her, bursting into the small shack and startling those who were within.

THE FAITH OF A BRIDE

There he found a pale and sweat drenched Tabitha lying in bed as several women and the city physician stood around her.

"Tabitha," Amulek's voice conveyed every bit of worry that encompassed him. Stepping between the women, he knelt at her bedside and grabbed her hand. "Tabitha, what is wrong? What has happened?"

Tears cascaded down her cheeks, and she gasped for breath. Unable to speak, she shook her head and turned away from him.

Amulek's eyes sought the doctor's. "Tell me what has happened."

The man sighed and walked over and rested a hand on Amulek's shoulder. "She will recover, Amulek, but the babe is gone."

Amulek froze. *What? The babe? Gone? He cannot mean it. Only a week ago we rejoiced in the news of our new life. How can this be?*

"I am sorry, Amulek." With a shake of his head, the doctor walked out of the shed, most of the women following in his wake.

Amulek's chest heaved as he sought to slow down his heart and he turned his face back to Tabitha. "Tabitha, dear one. Look at me."

Her shoulders began to shake as she cried, but she followed his directions. "I am s-so sorry, Husband. I have failed you. I have failed." Her face scrunched up, and she broke into sobs, her entire body lurching with the strength of it.

"Tabitha... Tabitha," Amulek reached out and grasped her upper body in his arms. Leaning over the bed, he held her. Whispering soothing words even as his own heart broke into pieces. He let his tears fall, saturating her hair as he wept over their lost baby.

"You have not failed, my love. It will be alright. All is well, all is well." Over and over he whispered to her. Words of comfort and love as they grieved together.

Hours later, after Tabitha had fallen asleep against him, Amulek raised his weary head at the sound of a knock at their door.

"Come in," he said softly.

Kezia poked her head inside the space, then walked on silent feet toward them. "How is she?" Amulek's mother wrung her hands at her middle, her face red and eyes bloodshot. It was obvious she, too, had been crying at the loss.

Amulek's heart went out to her. *She knows what it is to lose a child. If anyone understands it is Mother.* "She is exhausted, but the doctor said she will recover."

Kezia nodded. "What can I bring you? Are you hungry?"

Amulek shook his head. "I thank you, Mother. But I believe right now we need rest." His hand began to stroke down Tabitha's hair, a motion that was as soothing to him as it was to her.

Kezia nodded and bit her lip, but a tear trickled down her round cheek, anyway. "It is difficult, Son, but we love you and will do all we can to help."

Amulek forced a smile nodded his thanks. "I know you sorrow as well, Mother. Thank you."

With one last nod, Kezia backed out the door and shut it behind her.

TABITHA'S EYES FELT gritty and her body heavy. As consciousness came back to her, so did the soul crushing weight of her failure. Sucking in a large gulp of air, she pushed herself upright and surveyed her dark surroundings.

"I am here, Tabitha," Amulek's weary voice called to her in the darkness.

"Amulek?" She sought his form, grasping his hand as he reached for her.

"I am here," he said in a soothing voice, shifting himself closer to her.

Tabitha breathed a sigh of relief when she snuggled into his warm embrace. Yet, even as his presence soothed her, she nearly buckled under the shame. "Amulek... I am so sorry. I-I..."

"Shhh... my love. I know. I know." He spoke into her hair. "It is not your fault."

Tabitha's bottom lip trembled, and she grasped her husband tighter.

"Can you tell me what happened?"

She squeezed her eyes tight, wishing she could forget the day's events, but knowing it would be forever burned in her memory. "I was gathering the soiled linens, as your sisters and I often do." She paused to take a shuddering breath. "I have been having dizzy spells, which your mother assured me happens often when one is with child." She swallowed, striving to wet her dry throat.

Amulek shifted and stood from the bed.

Tabitha felt the loss of his heat acutely as she waited to see what he was doing. Moments later, a small flame sent a warm glow into the room and allowed her to see Amulek pouring water from a jug in the corner.

"Thank you," she murmured as she accepted his offering and quenched her thirst. After he had settled back beside her, Tabitha continued. "All was as usual until I bent over to pick up some wet bedsheets." The tears began dribbling unheeded down her face again. "A sharp pain in my belly brought me to my knees." She took a deep breath. "Your sisters helped me to a seat where I rested, but the pain came again, stronger this time. Leaving the laundry behind, Hephzibah and Mara nearly drug me back to the house, but as we entered, a great pain ripped through me and I..." Her voice dropped to a whisper. "I lost the babe."

Amulek buried his face in her hair and pulled her tighter into his embrace. His shoulders shook as he cried with her.

"Your mother brought me to the confinement shed and took care of me while one of the maidservants fetched the physician. It was over by the time you arrived." Tabitha's voice was thick with tears as she finished telling the tale. "I had such dreams, Amulek. I dreamed of giving you a son. Of giving you a child to be proud of and pass your legacy to. And now those dreams are gone." She broke down again, soaking his robe. "It is my fault."

"No. No, my Tabitha." He grasped her face and pulled her back so he could look into her eyes. "You are not to blame. Nature often takes its course. My mother was as you." He used his thumb to wipe her tears.

"She lost two babes after having me and still had my sisters." He leaned in and kissed her forehead. "Shh... my love. There is yet time. Do not lose hope."

Warmth spread through her at his sensitive words, but it was difficult to take them to heart. "How do you not find fault with what I have done? A woman's job is to bear her husband's posterity. I bring shame to your household."

"I, too, looked forward to the child of our creation, Love. But there is much time for us. We can try again. One day you will yet be a mother."

"But how can you be sure? How can you have such faith?" Tabitha looked into the handsome face of her husband. *Truly I am more blessed than any other woman.*

Amulek shrugged. "It does no good to focus on the negative. That will not help us accomplish what we wish." He hugged her to his chest. "We will have faith together. Today we mourn. But tomorrow we shall push forward."

With a weary sigh, Tabitha nodded her answer. *Hope. We must have hope.*

CHAPTER 6

6 Months Later

Amulek slipped out of the small building and quietly closed the door behind him. Leaning his back against the stone wall, he sighed and rubbed at his eyes which were tired and swollen.

"Is it done?" Giddonah asked from where he stood a few feet away.

Amulek jerked upright and turned to his father. Taking a shaky breath he nodded. "Yes. She has lost another one."

Giddonah scowled. "A wife should bear her husband a child. She is bringing ridicule to this house. What will our friends and neighbors think if she does not bear you a son?"

Amulek's jaw dropped. "How can you say such things, Father? Tabitha is nearly overcome with grief." He pointed a finger at the door he just exited. "Her body is near to broken from having lost these two children and you worry about what others think?" Amulek shook his head in disbelief. "Even you cannot be that hard."

Giddonah stuck his chin in the air and his eyes hardened. "She has not fulfilled the purpose of her womanhood. If you are left without an heir, our line will stop. What will we do then?"

Amulek stormed toward his father. The only thing that was keeping his voice low was his sleeping wife on the other side of the wall. "If we are left without an heir than we will pass on our heritage to one of our kindred. No one will think anything of it. There is no shame here. Tabitha has sacrificed herself twice now, and it is killing her. I will not hear another word against her." Amulek stepped past his father and began to leave.

"Perhaps you need another wife, Son. One who can perform her duties."

Amulek turned around, a muscle twitching in his jaw. "I will hear no more of this. Honor my request or I will leave, Father. I care not for what society will say. This subject is done."

Giddonah's nostrils flared and Amulek knew his father was angry, but Amulek's threat had not been idle and there was no doubt in his words. "It is on your head," Giddonah ground out before storming away.

Amulek rubbed his hands over his face, weariness hitting him once more. Forcing his legs to move, he walked to the sitting area and fell into one of the chairs. He faced the window and stared but did not see.

Movement sounded from his right, but he did not bother to look. The swish of robes settled on a chair close by.

"How is she?" Kezia asked quietly.

"She is resting."

"Is there anything I can do?" she ventured after a few moments of silence.

"Nay, Mother. The doctor has taken care of her and left. She needs rest for now." Amulek's mind whirled as he thought of his talk with the man of medicine. "He said…" Amulek swallowed hard. "The doctor spoke to us and informed Tabitha she may never bear children. He explained that having lost two is a bad omen." Tears clogged his throat, but he refused to let them fall. *Tabitha sheds enough tears for the two of us. I must be the strong one.*

Kezia clucked her tongue. "I gave birth to two children after losing two. There is still hope."

He heard her stand.

"I know it hurts, Son. It is a pain that never truly goes away, but time helps the ache. Be patient. Time will tell us the outcome."

"She is hurting, Mother. She is hurting and I cannot fix it." Amulek felt a sharp jab in his chest. "I can ply her with clothes and jewelry. I can give her anything money can by. But I cannot stop her hurt. I do not even know where to start."

Kezia walked closer and put her hand on his shoulder. "Love her, Son. Love and patience are all that will help now. Do not let her go through this alone."

Amulek nodded but stayed silent and eventually his mother left the room. Amulek's heart felt bruised and broken, but his eyes felt dry. His emotions seemed numb as he thought on the doctor's foreboding prediction. *What if she can never have children? What if her body continues to go through this horrible pain every time we conceive? Is there no way to cure what ails her? If we never have children will Tabitha still be able to find joy in her life? Should I consider my father's suggestion of another woman?*

The last thought caused Amulek to shake his head. "No," he whispered into the empty room. "I will never find another like her and do not wish to." He sighed and rubbed his hands down his face. "We will take what comes. That is all we can do. And if necessary, we will find joy in each other."

TABITHA FELT AS IF her chest had an unending hole in it. She lay on her side in the bed, curled into a ball, hugging a pillow to her body. Her tears had dried hours ago, but their therapeutic value had ceased long before that.

The day had passed and the small shed was dark. She could hear Amulek's steady breathing behind her and despite her hurt and anger, she found his presence soothing.

Her mind refused to let her sleep, however, as the words of her father-in-law played on a never-ending loop.

"She is bringing ridicule to this house... Perhaps you need another wife."

The thought of Amulek taking on another woman drove a spear straight through her. She knew that there were men who had more than one wife, but Tabitha had always hoped to be the one to hold her husband's affection. *Perhaps, I am too selfish. If I cannot provide him with the posterity he needs, then I need to be willing to let him have that with someone else.*

Even as she forced herself to think the words, they caused pain. She and Amulek had gotten to know each other in the last year and almost all her dreams had been fulfilled in their love story. *The only thing missing is a child.*

She sniffed as her eyes refilled with tears. *How can there be any left? I have shed so many.*

Warm arms wrapped around her from behind. "Shh... my love. All will be well. I am here." Amulek's voice was deep and raspy, making it clear he had been woken from sleep.

"I did not mean to wake you, my husband. Forgive me."

"There is nothing to forgive. Can you not sleep?"

"No. I..." She debated whether to speak her mind.

"Tell me, Tabitha. You know I wish you to speak your thoughts."

"I heard your father and you today, after I lost the child."

There was a long pause and Tabitha held her breath as she waited for him to respond.

Amulek gave a long, weary sigh. "I am sorry you heard that. My father was upset and did not know what he was saying."

Tabitha spun and faced him in the dark. "Will you follow his wishes and take another wife?"

"No," Amulek said harshly.

Tabitha jerked back at the sound and Amulek's body immediately softened.

"Forgive me. No, Tabitha. You bring no shame to me. I do not wish for another woman and do not want you to fear you will be replaced. I love you." He kissed her forehead. "What will be, will be. I know you are hurting. My heart beats with yours and also mourns at our losses, but I will not give up. If we never have posterity, then we will find happiness in our lives, regardless."

The hole in Tabitha's heart could still be felt, but the sharpness was softened at his words. "Has ever a woman been so blessed in her husband?" Tabitha reached out and rested her trembling hand on his bearded cheek. "I love you as well, Amulek. Thank you for your patience and your gentle spirit." Her voice was thick with tears and she began to shake as gratefulness overwhelmed her already exhausted body. "Perhaps there is a god we can offer sacrifice to? King Mosiah preaches of a god as well as many others. Is there something more we can do?"

Amulek stiffened and Tabitha paused, a frown marring her features.

"No, dear wife. That is not for us. We will be as we are."

Confusion at his words flitted through her, but Tabitha pushed the sensation aside. Her emotions were already too wrung out to handle anything else right now. "As you wish, Husband."

Amulek nodded. "It is well." Gathering Tabitha close, Amulek pressed a kiss to her forehead and held her long into the night.

CHAPTER 7

Amulek was grateful for the light, spring breeze that flowed over his face today. The last winter had been particularly harsh as his family had continued to struggle emotionally with the trials they suffered. However, hope was on the horizon and Amulek clung to it with voracity.

His mind often wandered to the night almost a year ago when Tabitha had asked about a god. He shook his head as he helped plant the fields. *No. My ancestors may have believed in the almighty, but I am content where I am.*

Standing, Amulek put his hands on his hips and bent backwards, stretching his back from the labor he performed.

"Amulek! Amulek come quickly!" Mara's screech carried along the breeze and clear across the field.

Amulek jolted from his reverie, picked up his robes and ran to his sister. "What is it? Is Tabitha all right?"

Mara gasped for breath from her speedy run. "You are needed-"

She didn't get the chance to finish her words before Amulek took off. Racing to the confinement shed, Amulek did not knock, but burst through the door. "Tabitha!" His voice boomed against the wooden walls, startling the servants who were working.

Kezia rushed to meet him, pushing him back outside and closing the door. "Hush, my son! Calm yourself!"

Amulek's chest heaved and sweat dripped down the side of his face. "Tabitha. Is she well?"

Kezia gave a small smile and nod. "It is almost over. You must have-"

The startling sound of Tabitha's scream made Amulek gasp in panic, but it was the baby's cry that followed that sent him to his knees. On all fours, Amulek sucked in oxygen at an alarming rate. "She did it. She did it!" Using the outer wall for support, Amulek climbed to his feet on trembling legs.

He glanced at his mother who had both of her hands over her mouth and tears streaming down her wrinkled cheeks. Their eyes met in mutual compassion and understanding. "Go to her," Kezia whispered through her tears. "Go to her and rejoice in this gift."

Amulek could only nod as he stumbled through the doorway, his eyes seeking Tabitha's.

The room was in chaos as the midwives bustled about, cleaning up and going about their duties, but it was the sweat drenched woman lying in the bed that Amulek was focused on.

Tabitha's eyes met his from across the room and lit up with joy. "Amulek," she mouthed, holding out her hand.

He smiled widely and started to step into the room when one of the women stopped him. "Please wait, Master, we are not yet-"

"I will not be kept from her," Amulek said bluntly. His eyes darted to the midwife's for a moment, but then went straight back to his wife. "I will see her now."

Lowering her head, the woman stepped aside and Amulek took a few long strides until he reached the bed. Sitting gingerly on the edge of the mattress, he leaned over and kissed Tabitha's forehead. "Are you well, Wife?"

Tabitha sighed at the contact and nodded. "I am. And I have a gift for you." Another woman walked over to the bed with a smile on her face and a wrapped bundle in her arms. Carefully, she set the baby in Tabitha's arms. "Congratulations, Master," she murmured before backing away.

Tabitha's hands shook as she pulled back the blankets so Amulek could see. "I have born you a son, Amulek." Her watery eyes went up to his. "A son," she whispered again.

Amulek's eyes went back to the red, wrinkled face of the child. "A son," he said in awe. "Tabitha... you are truly a gift." Leaning more fully onto the bed, he wrapped one arm around his wife and the other around the child, holding his tiny family in his arms. "I love you, Tabitha," he said as he kissed the side of her head. "I am truly blessed to call you mine and now we will raise a posterity together, which will only increase our joy. Thank you." Leaning up, he kissed his son's forehead tenderly.

Tears streamed down Tabitha's cheeks as she lay in Amulek's arms. "What shall we call him? Should we name him after his wonderful father?"

Amulek narrowed his eyes as he studied the child. "Nay. But we will call him Aminadi. One of my ancestors who was a strong and mighty man. And we will raise our son to be the same. He will bring great happiness to this house."

Tabitha nodded her agreement and sighed again as she ran a finger along the boy's downy cheek. "Do you wish to hold your son?"

Amulek hesitated a moment before nodding. One of the women still in the room rushed over and helped transfer the boy in to Amulek's arms. The child gurgled a moment before settling contently against his father's chest.

Tabitha lay her head back so she could see her son, but her eyes fluttered from weariness.

"Sleep, my love," Amulek murmured. "You have done well, and I am here."

Together, the trio closed their eyes and ignored the hushed sounds of the women in the room. Amulek fell into a peaceful sleep, knowing everything he wished for was in his arms.

THE END

AUTHOR NOTES

Thank you so much for reading this little story! I hadn't originally planned to write this part of Tabitha and Amulek's story, but as I planned out "The Faith of a Wife", I felt like something was missing. So, this short story of their marriage and love was the result.

It's easy to see I took quite a bit of artistic license as I brought these two together, so I hope you'll indulge my romantic side as I am a sucker for happy endings.

If you enjoyed this story, you'll love the next book, which starts fifteen years later, after Tabitha and Amulek are well settled. "The Faith of a Wife" follows their journey through the discovery of the gospel and Amulek's preachings and travels with the prophet Alma.

Again, thank you for taking the time to read my story. I love hearing from my readers and would enjoy knowing your thoughts! You can find me at:

lapattillobooks@gmail.com
facebook.com/lapattillo
Happy Reading!
L.A. Pattillo

OTHER BOOKS BY L.A. PATTILLO

Women of Faith Series
Prequel: The Faith of a Bride
Book #1: The Faith of a Wife (available for pre-order)
Book #2: The Faith of a Queen (TBD)
Book #3: The Faith of a Servant (TBD)
Book #4: The Faith of a Mother (TBD)
Book #5: The Faith of a Daughter (TBD)

Made in the USA
San Bernardino, CA
30 October 2019